To Rachael

Marjorie S. Barker

For Garry — M.B.
For my parents, Masao and Emiko Kogo — Y.

Text copyright ©1989 Marjorie Barker.
Illustrations copyright ©1989 Yoshi.
Published by Picture Book Studio, Saxonville, MA.
Distributed in Canada by Vanwell Publishing, St. Catharines, Ont.
All rights reserved.
Printed in Hong Kong.
10 9 8 7 6 5 4 3 2 1

Library of Congress Cataloging in Publication Data
Barker, Marjorie.
Magical hands / Marjorie Barker ; illustrated by Yoshi.
Summary: William secretly does the morning chores for each of his
three good friends on their birthdays, and when his own birthday
comes he finds himself rewarded.
ISBN 0-88708-103-7
[1. Work—Fiction. 2. Birthdays—Fiction. 3. Friendship—Fiction.] I. Yoshi, ill. II. Title.
PZ7.B250527Mag 1989
[E]—dc19   89-31373

Ask your bookseller for these other **Picture Book Studio** books illustrated by Yoshi:
Who's Hiding Here
Big Al by Andrew Clements

MARJORIE BARKER

Magical Hands

YOSHI

Picture Book Studio

William was a cooper, a barrel-maker. Six days a week he got up at sunrise and went out to his workshop. All morning he pulled long oak boards off the stockpile in his yard, sawed them into shorter lengths, and stacked the wood into orderly piles. All afternoon he carefully shaped the boards and fitted them together into strong barrels of different sizes. It was hard work, but William was a burly, no-nonsense fellow, and it suited him. And when people needed to buy snug, secure barrels for shipping or storing just about anything, they knew where to come.

William had three good friends who had shops on the same street as his cooperage. Every day they took time off from their work to have lunch together. One summer day, they sat together at a rough wooden table in the little restaurant where they always met at noon.

"Tomorrow is my birthday," said Vincent. He was as round and rosy-skinned as one of the apples he sold every day in his store. Friendly, cheerful Vincent knew the names of all the children who came to his fruit stand.

Philip leaned back in his chair. He owned the general store across the street, and his well-worn shopkeeper's apron was hung over the chair's back. "A birthday should be special!" he said. "But tomorrow you'll have to work, just like any other day. Wouldn't it be wonderful if there were some magical tool that worked by itself? Then on our birthdays, we could just command it to do our jobs!"

"That would be lovely," Vincent agreed. "I wouldn't have to spend half my birthday stacking up all the fruit into tall piles. For one day, I could just sit at ease by the shelves and enjoy my customers."

"And I," proclaimed Philip, "might at last be able to get my front windows washed." The four friends laughed together. Philip's store was so full and so busy that there was always dust somewhere, and he never had time to wash his store windows.

Adrian was the town's baker. He smoothed his black moustache between his fingers. "For one day, not to have to knead all my dough, and shape it into loaves and little rolls. To be able to just push it into the oven!" He, too, leaned back lazily in his chair, just thinking about it.

William smiled at his three friends. They were such dreamers! "Yes, it would be nice to have such tools," he put in gruffly, "but we all know it's just a silly idea."

Back in his own shop later in the day, William was still thinking about what his friends had said at lunch. He held out his two strong, rough hands. Perhaps there were no magical tools to help them, but he had all that he needed to make a birthday wish come true for each of his three friends.

William got up while it was still dark the next morning and went quietly across the street to Vincent's fruit store. He opened a box of yellow pears and slowly, gently, built a pyramid of fruit as he had seen Vincent do many times. When the pears were gone, William began to pile up shiny red apples; then he took the cover off a basket of fuzzy peaches and carefully arranged them in another stack. Sunlight was just beginning to show the outlines of the rooftops as he placed in order the last of the many different kinds of fruit. He slipped back across the street to have his breakfast.

Vincent was beaming at lunchtime. "Can you imagine!" he said. "All of my fruit was in beautiful towers when I went to work today! It's like our wish of yesterday came true! Now, William, you can't say that it was just a silly idea."

Smiling, Vincent looked around at his three friends. William tried to look just as surprised as the others.

The four friends relaxed as they enjoyed fresh wheat bread and steaming bowls of potato soup. This was Vincent's birthday celebration, so they took a little longer than usual with their meal.

William smiled as he went about his work that afternoon. That Vincent...talking as if some magic had made his wish come true! This was going to be more fun than he had thought it would be.

Several weeks later was Philip's birthday. Once again William woke up very early, and his feet crunched the leaves on the sidewalk as he walked through the quiet night to his friend's store. He brought two big buckets, one filled with soapy water, the other with clear water for rinsing.

William started on the outside of the store. The glow from a bright, full, autumn moon helped him be sure he got all the window panes completely clean. Then he moved inside. As he was using a soft dry cloth to polish the glass, the moonlight fell on a dusty stack of white china bowls nearby. William turned one over gently in his big hands. It had small blue flowers painted around the rim. He polished it with his cloth, pulled a few flowers from beside the doorstep, and set the dish filled with flowers on the windowsill. Then he headed home, stretching his arms and shoulders as he walked.

Philip burst into the restaurant at lunch time. "Do you know an amazing thing? I went into my shop this morning and my front windows were absolutely gleaming. And not only that, there was a lovely bowl of flowers in the sunlight on the windowsill!"

He looked at each of his friends. William tried to smile in exactly the same way as Adrian and Vincent, and to say "Happy Birthday" with exactly the same tone.

Adrian couldn't contain his surprise. "It's like some good fairy heard us wishing that day and comes to work for us on our birthdays!"

"Well, Adrian, your birthday's next," said Vincent. "We'll see if the magic is still working. Meanwhile, let's enjoy our lunch together."

"Yes," said William, glad to change the subject, "I think the fresh trout would be good today." It **was** very good, but William knew that best of all was having this special time with his friends.

William chuckled to himself several times that week as he thought of his "magical" powers.

He had to wait a while for Adrian's birthday. He looked forward to being the "good fairy" again! He laughed out loud in the early morning dark as he slipped on his clean blue work clothes and washed his rough hands in preparation for working with Adrian's dough.

His hands were accustomed to hard wood, and it was a pleasure on that chilly morning to feel the soft warm dough. It was more like working with wood than he had realized; cutting, shaping, smoothing. The rolls and loaves were soon resting in their pans, with soft cloths like blankets over the tops until it was time to put them in the oven. "Happy Birthday, Adrian," whispered William as he sneaked out the door, hungry for his breakfast.

That day at lunch it was Adrian's turn to be astonished. "It is true," he exclaimed, "there is a fairy who heard our wishes and that fairy visited my bakery last night!"

William shook his head.

When his own birthday came, William got up as usual and put on his worn work clothes and heavy boots. He clumped down the stairs and went outside to his workshop. He opened the shop door, and then stopped in his tracks: his wood was already sawed, sorted, and stacked next to the bench. The morning's work was done!

A grin slowly spread over William's face. The cool spring morning felt warmer as he thought of his three friends.

He walked back to his house and went into the kitchen. There on the table was a warm round loaf of bread, and a blue-flowered china bowl filled with strawberries.

William sat in his rocking chair by the fire, pulled off his boots, and leaned back. He bowed his head and sat quietly for a few minutes. When he opened his eyes, they were shining.

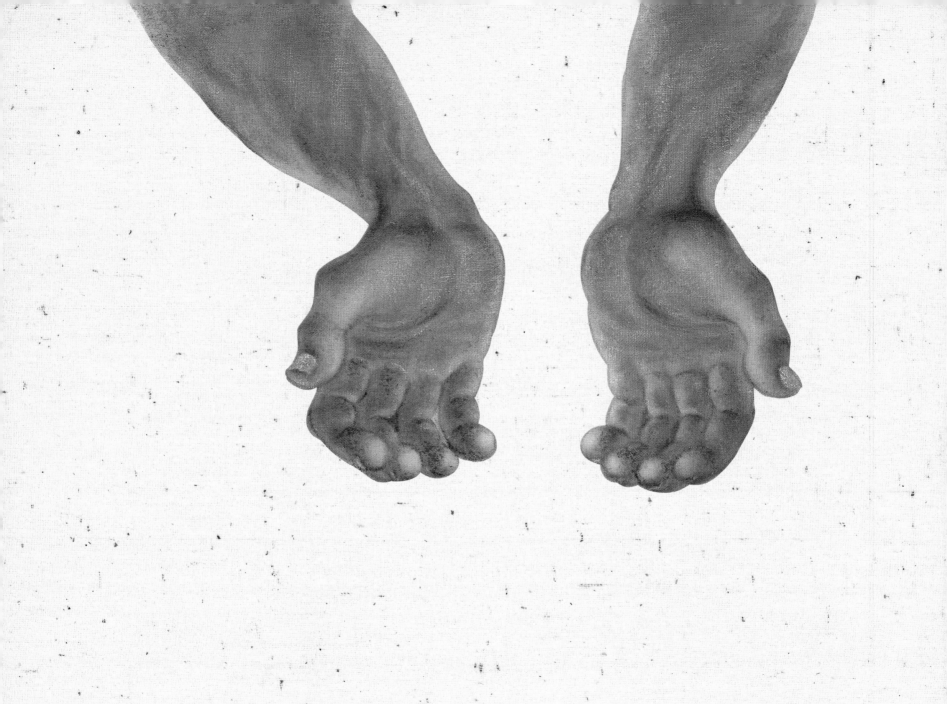

It is a wonderful thing, he thought, to have magical hands.